The Dark Spark
A novelette

Melanie McCurdie

Copyright © 2017 Melanie McCurdie
All rights reserved.

ISBN-13: 978-1977663832
ISBN-10: 977663834

MELANIE MCCURDIE

This is a work of fiction. Names, characters, businesses, places, events and incidents are either the products of the author's imagination or used in a fictitious manner. Any resemblance to actual persons, living or dead, or actual events is purely coincidental.

No part of this book, be it digital or hardcopy, may be reproduced or transmitted in any form or by any means, electronic or mechanical, including photocopying, recording or by any information storage and retrieval system, without written permission from the author

Greetings adventurer!

Before you begin, a few discretionary words:

Keep out of reach of children

Everything written from this point forward is to be considered snippets from my own twisted imagination and/or my own opinion.

The words that follow are not an official representation of any human, animal (warm blooded or cold blooded), extradimensional beings and/or biologically challenged individuals.

Actual offences or nightmares may vary from individual to individual. If conditions persist, stop reading. Some reassembly may be required. Batteries and weapons not included. Objects in mirror *are* closer than they appear.

Gratitude does not include tax, title, license or freedom from further subjection to bloodsauce.

Enjoy your read.

Melanie

DEDICATION

As always, for Muse,

For My Sweet Curmudgeon, Tom.

*For my friend and cohort James Saito.
Finer days ahead*
.

TABLE OF CONTENTS

Chapter 1 .... *Pg 1*
Chapter 2 .... *Pg 12*
Chapter 3 .... *Pg 22*
Chapter 4 .... *Pg 34*
Chapter 5 .... *Pg 41*
Chapter 6 .... *Pg 56*

ACKNOWLEDGMENTS

My gratitude to Christy Wright for providing her editing prowess and a brilliant idea for finishing this little tale. Thank you so much <3

Obsequiousness rendered obsolete
Eloquence is simply lost in translation
It astounds how little one registers
In the face of such tainted honesty
As though the paradigm shifted and
Reality had become a serial cannibal

1

When she opens the door, she wishes that she didn't have to step over the threshold and into the dark, cavernous shadows of that room. There is little choice in truth, but it didn't make the reticence any less a reality. The monsters must be kept at bay and they only way this can happen is to face the situation and face her fears.

"Get it together, Laurel." Taking a deep breath and uttering a small prayer, she does just that; around her neck is a small silver bullet that she holds firmly between her teeth as she steps inside to the musical tinkling of what sounds like thousands of glass bottles being jostled about.

It's not benign, what makes those happy noises.

The sludge that is contained in those glass bottles are the leftovers from the cleansings that she performs daily, the rituals she performs that help to keep the daemons trapped inside her at bay.

Stacked high on the shelves from floor to ceiling, the glass containers shimmer with a malignant glow. The bottles are the only way that Laurel has safely found to contain the small bitey bits of darkness that live on after she flays her heart bare.

It's not easy, what she does for therapeutic purposes, not when she bleeds as she does; the scars open as though they are fresh, every single time. It's alive, that soul sludge; it senses her, reaching out to press its finger on her sickened heart, especially at her lowest, as though it is singing her to hell.

This room, however, as much as she fears it, is home. Laurel loves to watch how it darkles, entranced by the way it dances and seethes along with the rage dance her monsters perform inside her soul. It is a pulsating closeness, snug as a hug, and it wraps her in its embrace much as a lover would wrap the object of its desire in its arms.

Just being in here leaves her breathless. In this room, she can see it all; everything is tangible, the beauty in the darkness that makes the shadows real and unashamedly, Laurel's eyes adore it.

Only in here can the visions trapped in her mind, the terrifying thoughts that in any other life would seek to drive her further off her moorings. A little batshit crazy, loosed in safety, is the only therapy she can afford.

"Maybe that shrink was right. Maybe I am ill," Laurel says softly, unaware that she is speaking aloud. It may also explain why Mama always said that she was almost evil and why that Priest kept coming to the house to cast out the devil Daddy insisted lived inside her heart.

The last time he came was the day Laurel left home. The Preacher said that she was the highway to Purgatory and that she may have been baptized into the Light but that she would always remain the blackest night inside. He said that she was born without a soul and then choked to death on tongue as soon as the words were uttered. Her parents drove her away and she has never looked back.

Something is different, though, and suspicion is King. The voices keep begging her to let them free, and she hushes them in a motherly, indulgent tone. *"Yes, my darlings, yes, my dears, soon,"* she whispers sotto voce with her hands clasped at her throat like a frightened child.

Laurel is no longer suspicious that there may be a problem. She is sure of it and it the knowledge scares her worse than any of the memory-like dreams trapped in the bottles and in the books. There is a leak. From the back shelves, a miasma slowly slips from its trap and is poisoning the room. The screams from that one canister are rocketing around the room, bouncing off the walls and rattling the other sleeping sarcophagi.

Their complaints tinkle in the din, shattering glass giggles as they touch one another. The shadows are deeper in the far corner, too, and Laurel watches them as they slither and lurk beneath the chairs in her work area. They sit in her chair, and slide their fingers across the keyboard, mimicking or mocking, perhaps both.

She can hear a sound, or sounds, from the one corner that Laurel makes every effort to avoid. That's where the vilest soup is stored. She doesn't go there, as a rule.

What truly frightens her is trapped in a box that she had shoved viciously into the hole under the shelves on the first day she entered what would become her sanctuary and her prison.

The box is still under the floor, but it calls to her, that box and if it is opened, and what is stored in it set free −Laurel doesn't want to go back there to see what is making that sound.

Somehow, she is already afraid that she knows what it may be and it calls for more consideration to safety than she wants to admit.

"I'll leave a message - send an email or something so that someone knows, just in case. Someone needs to be aware. The spirits of this place are more than ghosts; they are corporeal, solid, and yet made of smoke. They consume ravenously and while they eat you alive, make it feel like a lover's touch with claws of steel and as much as Laurel hates to admit it, the spirits are the ones that are in control here.

She worries that her message may not get through, with all the energy saturating the air she is breathing. The secret laughter from the bottles distracts - they are all giggling like lunatic inmates at the moon's apex.

The shadows are back at the keyboard; the figure they form leans in as its fingers fly, appears to nearly pant. "Is that what I look like?"

Laurel wonders, moving closer to the light of the monitor and feeling a shock thunder in her bones. The screen is filling with her words as she thinks them.

The only thing she could force into her mind while it reeled was an old tongue twister her 8th grade teacher had given her, "kiss him quick, kiss him quicker, kiss him quickest," and she gasped as it printed on the monitor.

"Oh, My Gods. What is this?"

She backs away, trembling from head to foot. Riotous thoughts of her loved ones' race through her mind; how will they know?

Would they believe what they'd heard, or would they know that she'd been trapped and was still here? She would just have to believe that they would know the truth and come for her.

"I am the ghost here," and the shadow mockery jolts in its seat when she speaks aloud before resuming its former posture. "I am the storymaker, and that makes me the one in control."

Behind her, a soft whimper derails her train of thought and she realizes that impossibly, there is a child here.

Laurel shivers, knowing that she is alone here and that there is no way that a child could have gained access to this room without her knowledge. She turns and is surprised by the presence of not a child but a young woman, one hardly old enough to be considered so.

The interloper's eyes are swirling white clouds fringed in lashes that look as though they are beaded in rubies. So mesmerizing, they startle with their beauty, and make Laurel recoil in horror all the same.

The changeling holds a freshly wound noose in her tiny hands and Laurel can smell the sweet scent of the hemp rope heavy in the air.

"Who are you? How did you get in here?", she snaps but Laurel gets no other answer than the sweet malicious smirk that twists the ingénue's lineless face. The youngster's delicate white hands flutter like doves as she tosses the rope at Laurel's feet, making her skitter back a few steps and her eyes widen when she sees that its noose has formed a crude heart where she had been standing.

The message is clear enough. \

The changeling shows Laurel her back; the skeletal string of her spine glows like a beacon in the dark, lanternlike luminescence coming from the racks and rows of soul soup, and Laurel follows, helpless not to.

Another figure appears from the dusk, lounging indolently against the shelf like a movie monster. The man's remaining eye leers, nearly slurping over her curves and she can't help but twist away and turn her head in disgust and fear.

His scent reaches her nose, burning it with a confusing concoction of rot and white roses; somehow repellent and attractive at once and all emanating from the punctured hole where his heart had once been. Laurel bows her head, feeling the weight of her own heart grow heavier under the weight of her own failures and tears.

The Changeling turns back; she has changed again, this toothsome chimera. She has become so much more beautiful and horrible - her flesh alabaster and perfect with curves that the eye was helpless to travel - softest flesh with hidden edges.

She holds out her hand, and Laurel watches as a ruby floats loose from her lashes to form a perfect, bloody tear that streaks that lovely face with crimson when it lands on her porcelain skin. With no hesitation, Laurel takes it, knowing full well her palm may soon be full of thorns or her fingers taken by hidden teeth.

Palms full of blood. Blood on her hands. "Gods, why must they talk in riddles?" she groans, pressing her thumb into her temple then stopping dead in her tracks.

"I am not going back there, not until you tell me who the hell you are, who he is and how the hell you got in here!" Laurel shouts, breaking the silence and brooking no argument. Her answer comes in the form of the business end of a....is that a Scythe? Who the hell is this bitch?

Laurel can't back away, or this twat will think she's won, and this damned thing at her neck is too sharp to shove away without cutting herself badly. She can feel the small pressure of its tip digging into her skin and determinately leans forward, pushing the ever-sharp tooth on its edge deeper.

Laurel stares back at the fool who thinks she can come into her place and make rules.

"Go ahead. I choose my own way. If I'm meant to die, so be it, but remember child, if I do, so do they." Laurel waves her hands at the racks and watches the Changeling's eyes transform. Her eyes are no longer white but an unnatural azure, and not something that Laurel would classify as part of the normal colour palette.

There is no shade in nature that comes close and nothing man-made either. They are hypnotic, the finest brushing of crimson around the pupil bleeds into purple and the most eye stabbing blue you can fathom.

The chimera smiles, turning her pretty face into a thing beyond imagining, and lowers her weapon.

Once again, the interloper holds out her hand, and this time, Laurel takes it with no hesitation. The strange beauty leads Laurel to the final aisle, there where the shadows are thickest, choking and nearly noxious in their nonexistence.

They swarm Laurel, enveloping and invading her throat as she attempts to scream, to run but it's of little use.

"I won't win this fight." Laurel considers the eyes of the one who led her here, and feels her grip let go on her hand.

The Box is open

2

Laurel doesn't know where she is; hell, she barely knows who she is, just that her name is Laurel Swindle and that this place is cold and it smells thick. The light here is far too bright and it hurts, even through her barely slitted eyelids. The best that she can do to alleviate the pain it causes is use her hand to shield her eyes and even that barely makes a dent.

"Did I land on the sun?"

There are voices, too, but they are muffled as though coming from under water. Male voices that are shouting both too loud and too soft to hear the words.

"Maybe I had an accident and my hearing was damaged, but that doesn't explain the lights." Prying her lids open a little further, Laurel realizes that the they are headlights and that she is on the ground, surrounded by running vehicles.

Inconceivably, it's night again and that alone is suspect. Laurel is entirely sure that it was daylight, and still early afternoon when she entered the writing room and now she has no clue where she is or how she got here.

There are men everywhere, it sounds like a ton of them too, all harshly yelling words she just doesn't comprehend. The light seems less blinding now and she can open her lids a little further without fear of them exploding - are those guns? Laurel's breath stops when she finally opens her eyes fully to witness four police officers, all with their weapons pointed directly at her head.

"Why are you pointing those at me?" she calls out, a little annoyed at the shrillness of her voice. Her hands tighten, the clench of her right fist curling slightly, and shudders when she sees what she's a had a death grip on. Oh. Oh no.

"Drop it lady! Drop it!" Several snarling voices shake Laurel out of her reverie and she can't help but sob at the sight of the knife; the way it shines in the headlights, waxing and waning out of focus. The blood on its blade.

Laurel drops it as directed, demanded and watches it turn in slow motion to land in a pool of what she had hoped was water. It isn't; water isn't that color in any world.

The weapon splashes lengthwise, kicking up a misty spray that lands like tiny cool ice chips on her overwarm skin. The wetness is both a blessing and a curse.

The tension surrounding her is thick enough to cut with – okay, that's not funny but apt enough. *"I don't want to be here."* Laurel whines in her mind, knowing full well that there is no way to change the outcome. All that she has is the tiny movie screen in her head that keeps playing and replaying the ghastliest sights imaginable and it's on a loop, making it impossible for her brain unsee or seem to forget. Faces with no names that haunt; they horrify and still, the images make Laurel salivate like Pavlov's mutts. *"What is wrong with me? It's her fault – that thing that I ran into, in my space. This is her doing."*

There is a voice at her left ear, urging her to stand in a kinder tone than she expects and a strong hand holds her upper arm a little too tightly to be friendly, all to assure that Laurel was indeed in some serious trouble.

The skin hurts under where his hand and the muscle burns and aches as though she's been burnt terribly. Glancing up, she blinks into a handsome face with a furrowed brow and full lips, watching her expressions warily.

Laurel is startled to find him so close. The scent of his cologne makes the daemon in her head chortle lewdly, demanding that she kiss him and see if she can get a little before they chuck her in the hole.

Admittedly, she is curiously considering it, until the milling men and women who are part of the cleanup crew behind his shoulder come into focus. Laurel suddenly can see the red, meaty mess that is laying there exposed. The ground is a soup of what she really hopes wasn't once human or animal but she is afraid that it is exactly that.

When the officer asks if she is well, Laurel pulls back in fear, both physically and mentally. She doesn't know what to say, so she nods, not trusting her voice to speak a lie. *"No dumbass, I'm not fine. I will never be fine again; the evidence points directly at me and so it should. I'm drenched and freezing in a coat of blood, discovered holding a knife, also drenched, and sitting in a – "*

Laurel shakes her head, hoping to rattle loose the monster that lives in her mind and to cease its constant whispering lies. "There is no way that I did this, I *couldn't* do this, not in real life. Officer, I might kill on paper, albeit virtual paper, but not in life - never in life!"

She freezes as the first body bags are loaded into the ambulance; "and yet - there are bodies, Ms. Swindle. Several it seems; the knife, the blood on your clothes and in your hair. So how do you explain that?" The officer holding Laurel's unrestrained arm lets go as they reach the door of the squad car , and offers a slight smile of reassurance before a covert flick of the eyes to his compadre in arms.

She wonders absently if it is a warning or a glance to see if he saw the smile, but she really doesn't know nor care. Without another word, he walks away abandoning Laurel shivering and feeling a strange loss as fear digs its claws into her throat and climbs down into her already weak stomach.

"Killer cunt." The voice is gruff, menacing, and full of evil delight. The other cop that Officer Handsome had flicked his eyes at; there is such an expression of nasty glee that crosses his face and drifts down to his mouth.

It turns what could have been a smile into a sneer when he hisses *killer*, all while twisting at his crucifix, and huffing that she should hang.

Hang. The rope. What is it with the Recluses and the damned riddles? He's right though, despite the less than acceptable wording.

"I *am* a murderess," Laurel spits at him, taking a deep breath in preparation of her next vocal outburst. She wants to throw it in his thick jowelled face, preparing explicative after explicative intended to stab deep into his gut like her knife had done to the blonde, but all that escapes is a gasp. Oh hell. "I remember."

"What's your name killer?" Policeman Piggy opens the door with a flourish then shoves her into the backseat hard enough that Laurel strikes the door handle on the other side.

Laurel's eye is throbbing in its socket and she snarls quietly, pressing the heel of her hand to the freshly bleeding mark on her forehead, desperate for some semblance of clarity. She is angry, and feeling her skin slide against the fresh blood, mixing it up with what is already smeared there makes it worse.

She thinks, *"I did this. Maybe I deserve to be manhandled and abused for it, but quite truthfully, I don't recall how, or why, yet. I need to buy some time."*

Policeman Piggy is leering into the open doorway, panting and sweating on the worn leather seat and demanding her name again.

"My name is Laurel Swindle, you fat son of a cunt. Think you have the balls to take me down or the ability to walk fast enough to catch me, if I run?

I doubt it, unless there are donuts involved. Close the fucking door. You're stinking it up in here." The bastard's face blanches and he slams the door hard enough to rattle the keys in the ignition and Laurel laughs a little to herself.

She knows that this isn't finished. Something niggles at her, intuition maybe; whatever it is, she is sure that more of what she's done will float to the surface like the malignant soup trapped in those bottles at home. Every other time, the leftovers had been kept safely stored away and the only horrors let loose were on the screen of her computer.

This time, it didn't stay there, and here she is.

Policeman Piggy stands with his back to the door. He's been joined by some of his brethren, and is laughing and glancing in Laurel's direction like a hero. He could use a lesson, she thinks. *"Like letting my knife slide into his back and then dragging it around to his well-fed gut. I could spill his intestines on his crappy ass shoes."* Pounds of noxious ropes splattering down in a bloodfall would be a just punishment for being an asshole. Listening to the piggy squeal would be like a symphony.

Laurel's body recoils, physically, but mentally she is aroused by the mental image, a lustful desire awakened that makes her damp with delight. *"Good job Laurel, you're coming undone. Unhinged. Pick your cliché but that's what this is."*

It's unpretty to beat oneself with the truth but Laurel knows that she has snapped and the evidence is everywhere. The iron bars of her control have failed. She can see that now but it's no damned excuse for taking a life, let alone however many poor souls she had managed to destroy tonight.

"Six. I killed six human beings."

But the first. She was beautiful, and knew it; her long hair was the colour of a raven's wing, and almost as iridescent. Laurel had wanted her and wanted to wind her fingers in it. She did, pulling Raven Hair's head back to expose that flawless flesh of her throat, as her other hand explored the contours of her body.

She begged for release, Raven's voice was breathless and like nails across the chalkboard. *"I gave her what she screamed for."* Laurel's knife had cut through the sweet-smelling flesh of her throat like butter just as she climaxed.

The woman's flesh split under its edge quite like her cunny had when Laurel's fingers found her opening and her blood was as hot from her throat as the juices are on her other hand.

"Gods save me; I did not mean to do this." Bullshit. *Yes, I did mean to do this.*

Laurel pushes her thumbs into her eyes and sobs when the white sparks start dancing behind her lids. She pushes them hard enough to hurt, to cause tears and stares bleakly at her reflation through the rear-view mirror.

Her skin looks raw under the streaks her tears leave through the blood, and her eyes are too wide to be anything other than shocked.

"I'm not a bad person. *I'm the worst kind of person.* No, I'm not. *Yes. I am.*"

The conflict in her head fades to the background when Laurel drops her gaze from the creature in the looking glass to have it land on a split in the wire wall that separates her from freedom. If she could pull the wires apart, Laurel would be able to reach the bag carelessly tossed on the front seat. The one that holds her knife.

3

A new voice in her head advises her sagely to wait and Laurel is agreeable to do just that. She smiles softly when two uniformed officers slip into the front seat and drive off without a word to her.

"If you could get your hand through, you could grab the knife and ram it into the neck of the meatsack driving. If you could reach it, you could shove its point into the base of his skull. I bet that you'll feel the tip crunch through all that bone and cartilage."

The new voice mutters conversationally and Laurel remembers the handsome ginger and the satisfying meaty grind when the metal sliced through to find its egress. The driving meatsack is watching her; his eyes narrow and his mouth spews curses and deplorable suggestions when he realizes that Laurel was returning his stare.

"You could suck your own cock. I'll help you, if you have one." Laurel retorts, smiling when they fall silent. "I will kill you. and no one will stop me. Or maybe I'll cut on you 'til you're ugly enough to make people vomit in the street, and leave you alive. Doesn't that sound like fun boys? Who wants to go first?"

They say nothing, and there is little but the babble of the radio until the piggy in the passenger seat points to a convenience store on the other side of the street. The meatsack stops the car at a convenience store, babbling about needing a piss and a fix and the other smirks and tells me that if I'm a good girl, he might give me a treat before we go to jail.

"Eat up Officer. Enjoy your last meal."

They didn't cuff her. Not initially and not now. Laurel is free to pull the split in the wire barricade wide enough to reach though and does just that. The skin on the back on her hand tears on the metal as Laurel grabs desperately for the plastic evidence bag on the front seat, next to all the empty donut boxes and chip bags. Disgusting.

She rips the plastic away; it feels like a prophylactic on her fingers, and all she wants is to feel the warmth of its haft, and smell the sweet scent of death soaked into its metal blade.

It feels like home in her palm, something akin to the touch of a long-lost lover, yet it had been only an hour since they'd last met. Laurel is nearly drooling with the desire to end the vileness of the demons dressed in human flesh and uniform. Her reverie is broken by the sound of cocky laughter, and it fills her throat with bile.

Laurel turns her head, slowly, so as not to jar loose the delicate glass ornament that she has imprisoned the tattered remnants of her humanity in. It would not do to have it loose, not with the way that it beats its fists against the fragile glass. Each hit threatens to shatter the membrane, as though screaming its demands to cease will change anything that has or will happen from this point forward.

The cop that was sitting in the driver's seat is now standing with his back against the door nearest her.

The window is open, just enough for Laurel to slide her slim arm through and to twist the blade deeply into his neck. She can smell the sweet fragrance of, the warm and salty blood sluicing under the surface of his skin. The daemon in her head howls at the pain in her brain; blind screaming pain as though someone has driven a red-hot iron bar into her ear at a thousand miles per hour.

Laurel throws the knife to the floor, the feeling of its cold and jellied handle is enough to ignite a burning boil at the back of her throat. "I refuse to do this. I can't do this. I'm not a killer!"

It wasn't me has never sounded more implausible. She didn't even buy the words coming from her lips. All the evidence pointed directly at her, accompanied by neon lights and brass bands, and there is no escaping those facts.

A soft giggle jolts Laurel from her internal argument and she realizes that the ingenue is with her; that woman-child that broke into her sanctuary.

She can't precisely see her, but knows that she is all around, filling the back seat with her presence and whispering pleasure into the cup of Laurel's ear with her fetid breath.

It's her fault. She did this. This thing put her in this horrible predicament, and forced her into a place where there is no escaping reality.

The Chimera vanishes and appears standing in front of the squad car with a sad smile and Laurel knows the truth with just a glance.

"I have two choices, neither appetizing," she thought, sighing. "If I choose the option that this terrifying beauty suggests, I'd lose me forever, lose everything that matters. My humanity would be destroyed, not that I had much use for it recently. Still I'd be bereft.

The other choice is to end myself, and then she can't make me do anything. The needs of the many, the safety of more than me outweighs. I don't want to die though."

How the blood sparkles like jewels in the early creeping shadows of the day.

The scant light coming through the car window turns the Changeling from some horrid thing to a work of art. Laurel shakes her head and returns to the problems at hand. The constants are the knife and the cop.

He matters for little more than a breathing test dummy in which to hone our skills. Laurel doesn't know his name but she does know that he is despicable, hardly better than she and worse, he hides his tendencies behind the badge on his chest.

At least I don't hide what I am, not yet. I know that am a monster but I feel bad about it. Laurel sees both sides of the coin now. The meatsack driver leans against the window, and his bulk blocks out what little light could reach her in this poor excuse for a cage. It's a bitch but he does her a favor by placing himself in the perfect position for her to reach through and thrust her weapon into his thick body.

The knife is home in her hand again, and she feels stronger when her fingers begin to slide in the blood of those who sacrificed themselves. Laurel folds her legs under her and rises on her knees, holding the blade down by the haft, its point down.

The rest of the herd is wandering off and I can see the last EMT slam the doors on the ambulance, then slam the flat of his hand against it to send it on its way. *"That might be a bit premature,"* Laurel smiles to herself, then rams the knife into the back of his neck, just out of his reach.

The cop shudders and splutters, fingers flexing and voice choking. All his cocky banter ceases and the silence is a pleasure to behold.

When he stops trying to speak, Laurel lets go of the haft, watching it quiver as he gags and gurgles, trying desperately to pull the knife out of his neck. The quiet is short lived when his buddies start shouting at each other to help him and still stand there frozen. The City's Finest indeed.

There is a dark-haired man leaning nonchalantly against a car not five feet away, with his arms crossed and wearing a bemused expression when the dying cop staggers towards a loose group of his gawking brethren. The poor man grabs the nearest of his friends, hands convulsing at the front of a freshly pressed shirt.

The odd fellow observing laughs out loud when the death grip is broken and his hapless savior panics and pulls away.

Her latest victim turns back to her, and Laurel can see the color draining from his face like a white line of sand pouring to the bottom of an hourglass. He is almost lovely in the sunrise with the bloodfall pouring from the tip that protrudes from the soft flesh below the shelf of his chin.

The way he trembles and quakes, then falters; he is like a graceless dancer, his life sliding away with each beat of his heart, each drop of blood that falls onto the dirt between his shoes.

Her handless door is opened with ease of leisure. The man that had been watching waves her out with a flourish and bows with a genuine smile; never being one to look a gift horse in the mouth, Laurel slides from the seat, hearing her flesh as it scrapes across the rough material. He glances at the cop, now lying dead between them with his blood staining the ground around him, and then back to meet Laurel's stare with an eyebrow raised.

It makes her feel like a chastised child, and even more so when he bends to pull her weapon from the corpse. There is a bubble and a belch of blood that splatters the skin further, followed by a wet grinding sound as it comes free.

Laurel stares at him, incredulously, trying to appraise whether this is a likeminded creature, or some sick joke. The stranger holds his hand out, the blade snug against his palm, and offers Laurel her weapon.

She snatches it from his prone palm hard enough to split the skin and the freak just laughs, hard and long, then licks at the wound with a wriggling black tongue. *"What the hell is this?* Laurel wonders to herself when he grabs her by the throat and slams her hard against the squad car.

"I gave you a gift, now you will give me one," the monster wearing a human suit hisses in her ear. His breath is fetid and full of enough rot to cause Laurel's head to pound harder than her heart. It sounds like the footfalls of the Devil himself. Laurel's face explodes in agony and she screams at the ice-cold fingers digging into her mind.

Positive she is about to die, Laurel lashes out, closing her eyes and clawing at the hand holding her in place in desperation to escape and her hands fall through the air.

The pounding isn't in her head; someone is at the door, fists falling like the hammers of Hell. Someone is at the door, and she is being killed by a Hellbeast.

Whoever is there, wherever she is, the voice on the other side is raised in anger or fear, which one Laurel is unsure but she wishes they would stop the noise. It's making her head ache.

The door flies open, slamming back with enough force to punch a hole in the wall behind it. Shadows fill the frame, menacing shadows that groan and growl and point with their clapperclaws pointed at her.

Suddenly the pressure is gone from her lungs and she can breathe again. The Bottles rattle and complain, sending the Room Recluses scattering, and their shattered glass giggles fill the already too full space with more noise.

On Laurel's laptop, words fill the screen; every thought, every feeling, every dark and evil action she had acted out was right there. A complete confession.

The Laptop pings, an email sent. "But, I didn't send an email. How could I? I wasn't here...?" Laurel moans to the Chimera standing near the open egress then sobs while digging at her eyes to clear the awful vision, when the changeling smiles with delight.

It's dark around her, the shadows are thick and comforting, almost numbing even as the yelling men advance on her. It feels like an embrace. Backing away from the desk and the intruders,

Laurel falls to her knees as her computer explodes, and shrieks when pieces of plastic and technology fly about her. The Recluses had saved her, and to feed their own amusement, they had also ensured she would be locked away.

The Changeling creeps closer and Laurel watches her perfect rouged lips part to speak.

Her voice is honey and whiskey, rough as a tiger's tongue but still offers some comfort nonetheless.

"Laurel Swindle, look deeper inside. Can you not see that it is a mirror? Look at yourself." Laurel knows that voice and knows better than to refuse, this time. A reflection. They made it a mirror and in its glass, is Laurel, drenched and freezing in a coat of blood, with that knife in her fist and grievously damaged eyes.

Oh Gods...it was real....

4

The fragrances in here are familiar, like home; the scent of birds in cages, despair, loneliness, and death. *"I don't belong here, not with these people, and not in a cage."* But I do and I am fully aware that according to society's laws, I absolutely do belong behind bars.

I have murdered several people, including three police officers but it was never in me to do those horrible things. It was *her,* the chimera, but they don't believe.me and there is nothing to do to change it.

Heavy footsteps alert me to a guard's approach long before he reaches the door of my personal enclosure.

"Who's there?" I call out, sliding further back, and feeling the bar that holds the bunk to the wall gouging into my back.

A deep voice greets my question, cool and concerned at finding me with my back against the wall, so to speak.

"Corrections Officer Jacobs, Ms. Swindle. Are you ready? Do you need anything?"

"I'm ready. I don't need anything, except for you to perhaps direct me the right way, Officer Jacobs." *I* hear the sliding click of the magnetic card slipping into the slot to unlock my door, and then the metallic clang of the bolt sliding back.

"Hands out. Feet shoulder width apart. I have a Taser if you insist on attempting anything. Do you understand Ms. Swindle?"

"Yes Sir, Officer Jacobs, I understand completely." What choice have I but have to comply, and I spread my feet, and holds out my hands, waiting to feel the cold steel against warm flesh. It comes, finally the burning desperation is quelled almost painfully by the weight of the shackles and the chain clinking as the cuffs are closed around my ankles and wrists. "I really don't want to go in there," I whimper with a shaking voice, but Jacobs doesn't flinch or soften.

"You have no choice." A hand firmly encloses around my bicep, not with malice but brooking no argument either, and he pulls gently so that I move forward a step, my senses adjusting to the limited movement afforded by my bonds.

"Yes, I know, but I don't want to. You've made a mistake, all of you. Please don't pull; I'm walking as fast as I am able to."

The jeers and shouts around me are disorienting as is the slight breeze of someone reaching out to touch my hair and missing. They greet me as I slowly move down walkway with Officer Jacobs guiding me further to the outside as we go. It wouldn't do to have me get too close to these degenerates.

All this hoopla makes me anxious and I hesitate slightly before he takes away my choice. "Come on Swindle. You're a badass bitch, are you telling me you're afraid of some parasite in a nice suit?"

If that were the only issue at hand, I would be cooler than a cucumber martini but it isn't.

The elevator hums as the doors slide open, a shush of air on my face and a damp, musty smell follows to assault my nose as I shuffle into the blurry box.

I've been in here before, too. This is the mode of transportation for the death row inmates. It reeks of cruelty and of death; the same black cloud that hangs over them all. "How many are going to be in the room please? I need to know."

Jacobs' hair shifts as he turns his head, the scruff of his beard scraping against the collar of his shirt, and I feel his eyes appraising me as he considers my question.

"Three. You, me and Mr. Trumble." I snicker at the name, and hear him snort softly in amusement just before the elevator shudders to a stop and the bell sounds.

More voices attack my ears, calling out my name; the sounds of clicking shutter buttons and rustling bodies like a congregation of carnivorous birds are cringeworthy. "You didn't tell me that the vultures were here," I murmur, lifting my hands involuntarily and feeling them stop as the chain's length reaches its limit.

"I'm sorry Laurel. I didn't know. *Open the door!*" he barks at someone and I again hear the lock disengage and whisper open. I can't help but shudder.

"Officer Jacobs, could you lead me to the chair? I can't see very well."

The bolt that slides home behind me as the door is closed makes me distinctly nervous, more so than the cut off voices from the hall which should have been much relief.

Instead, it made the sensation of doom all that much worse. Jacobs leads me across what feels like a huge room, stopping 31 steps in. He takes my hand and places it on the smooth vinyl of the chair standing there waiting. "Thank you."

The routine stays the same – I drag the chair back and take a seat, then hold my hands up so that Officer Jacobs can detach the long chain and attach another - I assume - to the table. I can hear the chain sliding along the surface. "Just your legs now. Stay still," he murmurs quietly and I remain frozen as he chains me to the floor. There is no hope of escape, not that I could get far anyway.

"It's very bright in here. The light hurts my eyes. Please, could somebody dim the lights? Something..." My request is met with laughter, incredulous and offended, hurtful.

"Let's talk first. A little light won't kill you, Laura, is it? Now will it?" Mr. Trumble, I presumed. Christ, he sounds young, somewhere around twelve with an ego the size of Texas.

"It's Laurel. Officer Jacobs, could you unshackle me so as least I can cover my eyes. It's painful, as you know." More laughter, mean, and not from the guard. This man is quite obviously an asshole that walks like a man.

"That's your name? Huh, at least it'll stick out in the press." he throws out, and I bristle, palms and neck feeling cool and clammy.

"I'm sure you have an assistant who has written in that file in front of you for you. Look it up. Who are *you?*" I bite back the queasy feeling that has been growing in my stomach since I was told of this meeting.

He scoffs, the spicy scent of his cologne makes my eyes water, and the breeze from the file as he flips it open flutters my face, followed by the scratchy sound of papers being spread apart. How irritating.

5

Trumble comes into sharper focus as he sets his chin on his clasped hands and leans across the table towards me with a smarmy grin plastered on his lips, "Tell me about it. I want to know what really happened. Tell me the truth and then I will give you the shades."

Aghast, I shake my head and in a low tone spit at Trumble, "What kind of sicko are you? Do you get off on the death and misery of others? Officer Jacobs, I'd like to go back now. Find me someone else to talk to because I won't feed this idiot's sickness." I stand again, and feels the Taser against my already aching ribs.

"Sit ... down. Do it, Swindle. I warned you once and I really don't want to hurt you over this dick," and I respond immediately, sitting and falling silent.

"I'm court appointed. Remember? You can't fire me. So, spill it," the parasite demands and I can't help but wish for his untimely death. Gods, what an ass this man is.

"I don't have to talk...," I murmur pointedly, quietly, and hear Trumble's breath catch as I peel the patch gingerly from my left eye, allowing him to stare into the empty hole where it once was. The horrified gasp and the low urk of his stomach trying to escape onto his lap was worth the ego blow.

The sunglasses rattle across the tabletop, one arm knocking against my knuckles. "Thank you. My eye is on fire and it still aches more than it should. I will give you some information provided there is no more mocking. Do we have a deal?"

The sun has shifted in the sky, and its distorted rays blurrily highlight Mr. Tremble's pale features as he nods his agreement. "Yes, Ms. Swindle, we do indeed have a deal. Shall we begin? For starters, how many others were there? Where did you meet them and what weapons did they use?"

Trumble's voice is steady and serious, and I am left stunned with my jaw hanging open.

Amazed at the stupidity, I can't resist chuckling a little in disbelief under my breath, finding his question ridiculous"

"Oh, so you think that the death of other people is amusing?" he indignantly throws at me, fury coloring his face and tone. This time I do laugh, right out loud, knowing full well that I'm risking getting my punk ass tasered and thrown into the hole.

Shaking my head briskly, and trying to gain control over my voice, I sigh again before trying to convey the facts to this stupid, stupid man.

"No, Mr. Trumble, I don't think that the senseless death of other human beings is funny. You seem to think my injuries are, however. Believe me, I got off lucky. What I do find amusing, however, is that you honestly think there was more than one perpetrator. No sir, there was only *one*. Weapons? Aren't you hearing me? Claws...*teeth?* Take a closer look, why don't you? 400 plus stitches to close the wounds alone. Never mind all that repair work that was needed inside.

Months of recuperation in this graciously provided government facility where *I don't belong*. Still think it's a joke? I don't."

He makes notes on paper. I can hear the small scratching of the ball point as it glides across the sheet.

"Sounds like a monster. What does it look like?" he asks, with a tone that is full of thoughtful laughter as he pauses, then begins tapping his pen against the table, vibrating on my already frayed nerves, "can you describe it to me?"

He is insane and I am surer of it now than I was when I first heard his less than helpful voice. *"What kind of lunatic thinks like this? This is wonderful; I'm behind bars charged with murder and they give me a psychopath for a lawyer. Jesus,"* I think with a bite and bark at him as loudly and sharply as possible.

"It sounds like a monster because it *is* a monster. Stop laughing, damn it! *It's not funny!* There is no other word for it - it just *is*. Call it a monster or the boogeyman or hell, call it Mother if you want, but stop making light of it!"

"Describe it to me. I want to hear what kind of sick fantasies your mind conjures up," and this time I snap, launching myself in frustration at the solicitor, at least as far as the shackles will allow me.

No matter the consequences, I am fully prepared to peel the smirk from his face with my fingernails.

Officer Jacobs sighs heavily and I feel the Taser dig into the skin under my right arm. The pain is enormous as everything becomes boneless, then rigid with the electricity coursing through my already tortured body. Agony flares in every muscle, each one thrumming; I am helpless to do more than groan and slump in the chair, panting as my mind wraps around itself to battle the enormous pain that has been inflicted on my sensitive flesh.

When I can find my voice again, I quiver and struggles for breath before pleading with Trumble for reprieve. "Please, do I have to? Isn't enough that I've seen it? Isn't it enough that I'll see it in my dreams for the rest of my life?"

The answer to my plea is evidently no and I realize it the second that Trumble laughs coldly and asks again for the story.

"Fine. Picture the most terrifying monster you've ever dreamt of, even as a kid, and now, make it thousand times worse. With claws. And teeth."

Trumble just stares, long and hard until Jacobs shifts behind me and coughs uncomfortably into his hand,

"C'mon Laurel. Stop the games and come clean so we can get through the rest huh?" I can feel Trumble's eyes trying to bore a hole through my forehead as though he can conjure the truth there for himself; fighting the urge to lash out at this fool once again, I find it simpler to just dismiss the question. "Bullshit. Try again," he barks, the sound of his chair scraping on the floor hurts my ears.

"You don't understand. It's not so easy to put words to, and you've already made it clear that you won't believe anything I have to say anyway," I point out to him, the steadiness of my voice surprising even me, "so tell me Mr. Trumble, what is the purpose behind me even speaking to you?"

"Try me."

I hang my head slightly, feeling that familiar burning behind her eyes again, and wishes that I could cry. "Alright, okay - It was human, almost. It stood on two legs, had two arms, fingers, eyes, a nose, tits and skin.

It looked like anyone you might see on the street or in the grocery store. Come to think of it, the creature was actually, sort of - attractive."

This earns me a raised eyebrow and a smirk, and I am encouraged, slightly.

"I didn't say that I was in love with it. Had it been human, I might have thrown a fuck at it but - if you didn't see it for what it is. If maybe, you didn't know what to look for, you would die innocent of the.... If...If I...may I have a Kleenex please?" There's a quick rustling and Jacobs shoves a wadded tissue into my hand. "Thank you. I wish I'd never seen it at all, and now I can never, ever forget."

Officer Jacobs is at my side again, this time with a comforting hand and a glare at my court-appointed Liar, "Haven't you heard enough?"

The Liar shakes his head and with a curt gesture waves him off. "Ms. Swindle, what exactly did you see? Describe it in detail, please."

How do you describe the terror of your life, both in waking and in dreams?

I could never make real for them what has plagued me and I wouldn't wish it on anyone, though if Mr. Trumble continued his current path, it was certainly an option.

"What did I see? I saw complete and utter darkness, there was no life there, and it was cold, dead. Then it turned around and I wanted to scream, to run and scream and never ever stop but I couldn't make a sound.

It had an angel's face; so, otherworldly that it was fearsome. Perfect glowing skin, perfectly shaped red lips, as though they were coated in blood. The hair might have been blonde but it really it could've been any colour. I didn't notice. What I did notice were its eyes. No, Mr. Trumble, you can throw me into an oubliette and forget that I exist, but I won't talk about the eyes."

Trumble simply stares and sighs, before stating baldly, "You are truly insane, Ms. Swindle." I can hear the rasping of his fingers as he runs them through what remains of his hair, and shrug my shoulders, knowing that no matter what I say to this man, it will make no difference.

He'd have to see it for himself and Gods; I'd never wish that on another human being, no matter how vile he may be.

"Do you want the rest of the story or have you made up your mind?"

He encourages me to continue with a curt wave. "Yeah, go on, and this time *describe* it," and I can do nothing more than inhale as the memory begins to fill the now useless sockets that I used to see out of.

"If eyes are the windows to the soul, then surely this creature's soul is a brackish black hole.

This thing was always insane and it sees us as vermin; we are little more than parasites to be exterminated. This thing wasn't born, it just is. I saw that in whatever passes for eyes. It was so cold in there, a wasteland.

If you saw.... I saw -there's not one ounce of humanity or sanity in those eyes. It holds you, and you can't fight it. You're frozen in place while it tries to eat you alive."

A muted crash further up the hallways interrupts the breathless recitation, and I startle, making the chains titter. Trumble explodes again, yelling at no one and loudly too. This guy has a serious anger issue.

"*Bullshit!* There's no such thing as being 'unable' to fight. Nothing can hold you like that. It was *your* choice, Swindle, and I can't help you if you won't be honest with me!" he screams, pressing his bare inches from mine.

I could have ripped the nose off with my teeth but Officer Jacobs is back at my side with his hand resting on my shoulder again, to calm me while placing his other between us.

"*It was your choice,*" he repeats emphatically.

I shrug his hand off as I attempt to recover from this latest verbal attack, and feels disgusted by the fine spray of spittle that is drying on my face.

"You don't have a choice. There is no choice. Listen to me. These shackles you have me in? They wouldn't hold it back. No one who has encountered this thing has survived, and you won't either unless you pay attention!"

Trumble snorts derisively and spits more of his venom at me while the noise in the corridor gets louder. "Listen up Buttercup. Finish your little soliloquy and let's get this over with. You have ten minutes then I'm out of here. Colour, impression, limericks. I don't care. Just spit it out."

"Color? Why does that matter? It's not like you can look at it for that long. It's a chimera, a changeling and it moves sort of like a kaleidoscope?

I know what you're thinking and no, I wasn't high, I know it sounds like an acid dream but it's not. This was and is no fucking dream; it is absolutely real and it looks like a woman. Mr. Trumble, this happened and it will happen again."

"Sounds like a threat, Swindle," the Liar intones.

His words are suddenly cut off when the high-pitched prison alarms begin to wail and shriek in my ears.

"No, it's not a threat. Please just listen. It nearly killed me when it escaped. It tried to eat me alive. I lost everything that day. You don't know what this thing is and you think I'm playing a game but I'm not. Why are those alarms going off?!!"

Officer Jacobs leans and speaks into the shell of my ear, informing me that there has been an escape and that is why the alarms are clamoring away. I shake my head slowly, knowing full well that it is a complete fabrication. No one has escaped; no, something has broken in.

"Officer Jacobs, Mr. Trumble, it's here. It's coming for me, and you have me bolted to a damn table and the floor while it's hunting me.

I saw what it really is, and it wants to kill me. Please, I don't want to die. Let me go!" Jacobs squeezes my neck tightly and glares at Trumble.

"I'm going out there. Swindle, you stay here, stay seated and do not let him bait you.

Do not make a move. I don't want to be forced into action. I don't trust *him*, so **you** be alert. I'll be back in 60 count."

I can feel myself breaking out into a cold sweat at his words, and try to catch hold of his sleeve before he can move away and miss completely. "No!! Please sir, don't leave me in here with him! Please, it knows where I am and it'll come for me. You can't leave me here alone. Please, I don't want to die alone! Mr. Trumble, what is that noise?"

The Liar doesn't respond to my increasingly frantic questions, choosing instead to breeze past to peek through the small window in the steel door; Officer Jacobs had triple checked it before walking away to his death or captivity, depending on its mood. *Gods, for his sake, I hope he is dead.*

There is a high frequency whine that makes Trumble cringe and causes my bones to quake in fear.

He hammers on the door calling for Jacobs, and immediately knows that he has just made a lethal mistake by calling for help.

I know that noise all too well. It's found me. *She* has found me and I have no way to save myself, not while chained to a bloody table with no way to free myself. *I don't want to die —* "

"Mr. Trumble, please, unshackle me. Why - what are you doing!? Please don't open the door!! How did you get the key? Jesus Christ on a coconut cupcake are you **crazy**?!"

All I can hear are the razor-sharp claws scraping along the walls, and the bloodcurdling screams emanating from not so far away. That alone makes me ill, but the sloppy sucking sounds are nauseating, almost as much as the watery intake of breath of Mr. Trumble when his eyes presumably land on the creature slaughtering the vermin the creature views as wasteful life. I hear him sigh the words, "so beautiful," as the talons slice the air just outside the open door.

There is a heavy thud of what I can only assume is his head landing on the floor and I know it without a doubt when the hair of his noggin brushes the leg of my pants as it settles at my feet.

6

One swipe is all it took. I am trapped, bolted to the floor, and its mind is already on mine, reading fear and lapping it up like a sweet treat. *"It sees me and I can't run. There is just nowhere left to go."*

The Changeling whispers my name in honeyed tones that are full of razorblades. "Laurel," it croons, smoothing my hair gently from my face with damp claws much like my mother had done when I was a child. "Laurel Swindle," it sighs, caressing my name like a lollipop, with its deathly sweet breath grazing my skin and it feels like lust and desire. *I am losing my sanity.*

I don't want to resist when it demands that I open my eyes, though I do, shivering against the pressure of its pinpoint teeth hard against my neck with a desirous groan. I really don't want to resist but do that, too, for a time, just to listen to it cajole.

Its words are poison; it's lips are on my throat and its claws tangled in my hair; strangely, it wriggles and gasps though in sexual agony.

I am paralyzed by panic, by fear and shake against the soft pressure of the ever-sharp claws brushing against the scars it had left me with last time. "Laurel, come with me," it coaxes, "you can be free, with me," and my eyes fly open when the chains fall away from my wrists and ankles like magic.

I can see again, see with both eyes and the world is so bright and vivid, almost too much not to devour. Even the bland interrogation room looks like a landscape skyline to my starved senses. The changeling has given me a gift and all that it wants in return is to be acknowledged. Despite the carnage that I know exists beyond these walls, it seems a small price to pay for freedom.

The perfect complexion, full lips, statuesque body; it has built such a stunning human-like form that even knowing what it is, that even I am helplessly aroused by the wide-eyed slack jawed expression.

Laughingly, it stares, almost as awestruck by my horrifically marked hapless beauty as every other human that has ever encountered *it* has become.

"You are so beautiful," the changeling sighs, turning to dust in my hands, "so - beautiful."

ABOUT THE AUTHOR

Melanie McCurdie is a Canadian based writer who resides in Murfreesboro, Tennessee. She is a Warrior Mom blessed with two challenging boys, Sam 15, and Davey 11. She is also a rabid supporter of Independent Film and Publications, and a horror junkie with a taste for pretty words, and bloodsauce.

Most recently, Melanie was voice talent to The Carmen Theatre Group as Maria Sanchez and she can be seen in The Orphan Killer 2: Bound x Blood, written and created by Matt Farnsworth.

Made in the USA
Middletown, DE
02 June 2018